CLASSIFIED

YOU CAN'T HIDE THE TRUTH FOREVER

YOU CAN'T HIDE THE TRUTH FOREVER

BREAK OUT!

TERRY DEARY

KINGFISHER

An imprint of Kingfisher Publications Plc
New Penderel House, 283-288 High Holborn
London WC1V 7HZ
www.kingfisherpub.com

First published by Kingfisher 1996
This edition published by Kingfisher 2007

2 4 6 8 10 9 7 5 3 1

A CIP catalogue record for this book
is available from the British Library.

ISBN 978 0 7534 1535 1

Printed in India
1TR/0507/THOM/MA/80STORA

Contents Page

Introduction

All governments have secrets. Sometimes these concern the activities of enemy countries, sometimes those of their own people. Just as often, however, they conceal the 'dirty tricks' of the governments themselves. These 'tricks' include both lying to friendly countries and spying on the military systems of hostile ones.

During the Cold War, the USA and Russia spent vast amounts of money trying to steal each other's secrets. To do this they set up the biggest and most technically advanced spy networks in history. However, such networks had one major failing: they were run by people.

People can be tricked, bought or blackmailed. They can be persuaded to change sides. They may even choose to work for both sides at the same time. Compared to computers, they're just plain untrustworthy! And many people handle secrets. If just one responsible person turns traitor, untold damage may be done to a country's national security.

So, you'd think governments would check every link in their spy chain. But too often they fail to. Would you be surprised to learn that, in the US in the 1970s, one highly-trusted 'link' was a disillusioned young man eager to make money and critical of his country's role in world affairs?

Incredible as it seems, it's true. The young man was called Mike Baines, and in 1977 he was jailed for selling 'vital' US secrets to the Russians. But doubts remain about Baines's crimes. Did the secrets he sold have any real value, or was he just a pawn the CIA used to pass on false information? Just what was in those top secret files? Files marked:

CLASSIFIED

CHAPTER ONE

"You're a *what*?" I laughed.

"A spy. I'm in here for 40 years. For spying." My cellmate turned from the barred window and stared at me. Not a muscle moved on his face.

I stretched out on the bottom bunk and stared right back. It wasn't just that he was so young. He was so *normal*. Middle height, good build, neat brown hair and a clean-shaven, good-looking face. He looked real respectable, like an accountant or a lawyer. Only there was something wrong with his eyes. They were dead, no-hoper's eyes.

"Forty years!" I whistled. "What'd you do? Shoot 007?"

He looked me over, weighing me up. "Spying isn't like you see it in James Bond movies," he said, real superior, and turned back to the window.

You see, I like most people. I'm *interested* in them. When I meet someone I want to find out all about them. It's just this thing I've always had. But over the years I'd learned that some people don't want to open up. When I made the crack about 007, I saw him switch off. He thought I was a wise guy, and he didn't like it. I knew I'd have to lay off on the cracks if I wanted to get to know him.

"Name's Larry Holtz," I offered.

"Baines," he drawled, like he *was* James Bond. "Mike Baines."

"I'm in for robbery and wounding," I said and watched a hint of fear flash across his face. "Hey, don't worry, Baines, I'm no psycho. I just shot at the cop who got in the way of my last bank job. He was just out of luck, turning up at the wrong time like that. Hell, I even apologized to the guy.

1

What more can you ask?"

Baines looked interested. "Did you mean to kill him?"

"I don't know. I honestly don't know. What about you? Did you mean to commit your crime?"

He frowned. "I don't really know either. I thought I did at the time. Now I can't remember."

"Want to tell me about it?" I said, casual as you please.

He turned back to the window. "Nope," he said.

He was going to be a tough one. But I had time. There were three whole months left of my stretch.

I got up and joined him at the window. In the exercise yard some of the cons stood in groups, some leaned against the wall. The ones I watched were the ones who moved from group to group. I saw who was talking to who, who were the messengers and who was running things. I even saw things change hands which the guards missed. They were all there below us like chess pieces on a board.

Mike Baines saw none of that. He was looking up at the burning sky. I squinted to see what he was looking at.

"Hey, Baines," I said. "It's funny but you always look up – I always look down."

Then he murmured something that seemed weird at first.

" 'Two men looked out through prison bars; one saw mud, the other saw stars.' "

I thought about it. I knew prisoners like that. Some try to see the bright side of prison life – some only see the bad. "Pretty," I said. "You write that poem?"

He smiled a little. "No. A guy called Oscar Wilde wrote that. A nineteenth century Irish writer. He ended up in an English jail."

I shook my head. "I wish I'd got me some education like you. You go to college?"

It turned out I'd pressed the right button. He began to

open up. "I went to a good high school for a while, a Catholic school – very old-fashioned. They didn't approve of Oscar Wilde, though we studied him. He was an outsider – he kicked against the system – that's the reason they locked him up."

"So where was this school?" I asked.

"Los Angeles," he said.

"The *rich* part, I bet."

He turned the corners of his mouth down in a sort of face-shrug. "Dad was in the FBI for a while. Then he went to work in the defence industry. We were never short of money, even with nine kids in the family."

"Nine!"

"I was the oldest," he said.

"So you went to college after high school?"

"I never finished high school. My parents moved me to another school – Rolling Hills High. They weren't too satisfied with my progress. My grades were dropping to C. After they moved me, I *really* lost interest."

I laughed. "My mother was happy if I scored Grade E. So I never disappointed her. So your parents moved you because of your poor grades?"

"No. Not just that. They moved me because of a guy called Curtis Jonson. He was my best friend..." he twisted up his mouth, "Curtis Jonson. But they moved me too late."

I took a wild guess. "Jonson is the reason why you're here, right?"

But he was looking out of the window again. "There are birds up there," he said.

"I guess there are," I muttered.

"Different kinds of birds, all flying free." Then he said another strange thing. "*I'm* not going to let them shut me in here for ever."

"Nope," I said. "You'll be out in 40 years. Maybe less – with parole."

"No," he said fiercely. "Sooner. Much sooner. I'm going to break out of here."

Chapter Two

I stared at him in amazement. The guy was serious! Shouts and laughter drifted up from the cons in the exercise yard. I'd heard escape talk from some of them. But they were tough guys. Coming from Mr Average here, it was pretty hard to swallow.

"Maybe I could help you out," I said, offhand, just making conversation. "I've only got another three months. But I hate the thought of a guy like you being stuck here for 40 years."

He didn't say anything right off, so I went back to my bunk. He was staring up at those birds again, poor sap. But then a weird thought came to me. What if I *did* help the guy break out? At most, I'd get a few months added to my stretch. Besides, I had a feeling there might be something in it for me. When *I* got out, Baines – wherever he was – might be feeling generous.

So I decided, next time the subject came up, I'd offer Baines some help.

Mind you, there were moments when I thought Baines wasn't all there, if you get what I mean. Like the time he told me all about his hobby. Let's just say it wasn't stamp collecting.

We were lying on our bunks after lights out, unable to sleep. Baines just started talking, *and* without any prompting.

"You got any real passions in life, I mean things you like to do more than anything else?" he asked. "I have." He continued, not waiting for an answer. "The thing I really get a kick out of is falconry. You know – taming hawks and hunting with them. When I was 15 I saw my first hawk close up. One of the guys from high school – a few years older than me – had left home to become a hippie. His name was Ed and he had a hawk called Majesty. One day he called at the house. He said he'd heard I was interested in birds, and asked if I would like to see his bird fly."

I didn't interrupt, I just let him remember.

"Anyway," he said, "we took Majesty out onto the hills overlooking the Pacific. The hawk had a hood on but he could hear what we could hear. The larks singing in the sky."

I had an idea what was coming.

"Ed stroked him and whispered to him and slipped the leash from his feet. Then he used his teeth to loosen the fastening on the hood. The hawk leapt into the air and climbed like a rocket towards the clouds. Ed and I ran across the field to send the nesting larks up into the sky. Majesty picked one out and then dropped like a javelin. The lark just kind of exploded when he hit it. He brought it back to Ed's wrist to eat. That beak ripping at the dead bird..."

"Terrific," I said in a monotone.

"You don't know how exciting it is till you see it for yourself. I've studied falconry over the years. Read every book ever written on the subject. It's the ancient sport of princes."

I bit back a reply about preferring baseball. I guess rich kids like him thought they were the princes of LA. "Bought your own hawk, did you?" I asked.

"Sure. I had quite a few. I spent every spare minute with them when I was at high school."

"Kind of lonely, though. Just you and the hawks?" I suggested.

"No! Curtis had hawks, too. Why, one of his red-tailed hawks flew clean into his face once. Buried its talons into his cheek. Man, when we were out with the hawks, we were *really* living."

There was a short silence in the bunk above me. Then he said suddenly, "That's why I called myself the Hawk."

"What do you mean?"

"It was my code name. For spying."

I almost wanted to laugh. It sounded so stagey, this spy business. I decided to change the subject.

"So, tell me about this Curtis," I asked.

"No, I don't think so," he said. And I heard him turning over to sleep.

Some jails have walls. Lompoc was more like one of those prisoner-of-war camps you see in movies. It was ringed by two three metre fences topped with razor wire, one fence inside the other. It was a high security slammer, specially for lifers, trouble-makers, and other high-risk cons.

Anyway, two days after our talk about the hawks, Baines asked me if I'd like to do some running on the track inside the first fence. Well, the only running I've ever done is from the law. He could run like a jack-rabbit. After the best part of a kilometre, I was ready for intensive care.

But with Baines's encouragement, I kept it up. Each run made me a little fitter. Soon I was able to keep up with him some of the way. The guards ignored us, and we could talk without being overheard. One day I'd been thinking about what he said about breaking out, so as I jogged I thought I'd point out a few things to him.

"See the space between the fences?" I panted. "That's... the killing zone."

"Uh-huh," he said.

"Each of the watchtowers has guards... with high-

7

powered rifles... there's no way you can climb even the first fence... without being seen and shot."

"Do they fire warning shots?"

"Sometimes... sometimes not."

I could see that got to him. He had a frown on his face the rest of the day.

"Listen," I said that night. "I really meant what I said about helping you break out – if you're still serious."

He narrowed his eyes. He was real suspicious. It was understandable: I might have been a snitch.

"What's in it for you?" he asked. I told him straight out I thought he might be able to help me on the outside. He didn't say anything to that, and we went to sleep in silence.

Each day we ran that circuit. I could see Baines measuring out the distances between the watchtowers and looking for blind spots. As for his question about the warning shots, it was answered soon enough.

We were jogging round the track clockwise while two other guys were going in the opposite direction. Guys from our block – Holmes and Winkler.

They nodded at us and I reckoned they looked a little nervous. Then I heard a clattering behind me. I stopped and turned. They'd started to climb the fence, trainers scrabbling at the links and fingers twisted in the wire. There was no call from the guards. The first we heard from them was the crack of a rifle shot.

The bullet caught Holmes in the leg and he tumbled over the wire into the killing zone. Then Winkler was hit in the shoulder. Both tried to make it across the dirt to the outer fence. More shots hit them in the arms and legs, bringing them down.

It had happened so quickly I realized I hadn't taken a breath. There was a minute of shocked silence. Then I turned slowly and looked up at the nearest watchtower. A rifle barrel was zeroed-in on a spot just above my nose. The guard was hoping I'd make a false move, and give him more target practice.

Stretcher-bearers ran out and carried the men off to the hospital ward.

I felt sick to my stomach hours after they'd locked the cell door behind Baines and me. "No warning shots," I said quietly.

"Maybe it's easier to escape from the hospital," he said.

I lay back on my bunk and tried to work out what he was saying. Then it hit me. "Are you saying Holmes and Winkler just wanted to be wounded so they'd end up in hospital? Listen, Baines, if that's your escape plan, forget it!"

"I'll think of something better," he promised.

CHAPTER THREE

Next day I thought I'd probe a little deeper. "You never did tell me how you came to be in here." I'd woken early and lain on my bunk watching the rays of the morning Sun coming through the barred window.

To my surprise, he answered straight off. "I'd no idea what I wanted to do when I left school," he said. "When I was a kid I wanted to be a teacher. But by the time I went to high school I was beginning to have doubts about everything in this country. And I began to have doubts about this country *too*. America the beautiful, America the free – it was free to bomb peasants in Cambodia and send its young men to die in Vietnam..."

There was a pause, as if he'd lost the thread of his thoughts. But then he went on with greater certainty.

"I decided to take a job and save some money before I went on to college. I thought I'd use the time to think about what I wanted to do. My father approved and through a friend of his, got me an interview with a defence company."

"Good job?" I said.

"Nope. I started in the mail room. Very low-level, very boring. But a job. Hundred and forty dollars a week. The mail I carried round the building was top secret. I wasn't allowed to look at it, of course, just deliver it and keep a record of where the files were."

"What sort of secrets?" I asked.

"Spy satellites," he said. "The company I worked for manufactured spy satellites. Satellites so powerful they could pick out and photograph a man walking across a desert. Back in 1971 they were so secret the public didn't even know that we had them up there in orbit. They could send information back to Earth about what was happening on the missile bases in hostile countries... Russia, China, Cuba and so on. You know what they called these satellites?"

"No," I admitted.

"Birds," he told me and gave a short laugh. "Those birds are up there right now, looking down on us. Seemed only right that a hawk-lover like me should be working with those metal spy birds."

"You never did any secret stuff yourself though?" I asked.

"Not at first. But after a while they thought I was suitable material for one of the communications rooms. They made me swear to secrecy, then gave me a job handling the information being transmitted by the satellites. Most of the messages coming through my machine were for people in the Central Intelligence Agency. They had the job of interpreting this information."

"Why couldn't the messages go *straight* to the CIA?" I wondered.

"Because the receivers weren't in the US," he told me. "They were in the heart of Australia. I was the link between Australia and the CIA."

"And those were the secrets you stole?" I asked.

He didn't reply, but eased himself down off his bunk and went to the window. "Come here," he said.

I thought he wanted me to look at something through the window. I got up and walked over to him. He stepped aside to let me stand in front of him. In an instant he'd grabbed my hair and pushed my face hard up against the bars.

"What are you doing?" I cried. The more I struggled, the more it hurt. I relaxed and let him talk. He spoke quickly in a low voice, not wanting to attract the guards.

"When I wanted to catch a hawk I'd use a live pigeon. It would have a fine net on its back and a thin line attached to one of its legs. When the hawk swooped to catch the pigeon it got tangled in the net. I reeled in the line and captured the hawk. I set the pigeon free after that."

"Okay, okay, Baines," I muttered against the cold steel bars.

"That's how they tried to trap me where I was before, in Stone Island prison. They sent in a pigeon… a stool pigeon. An old Italian guy called Guido. I'd been found guilty of treason – spying on the USA – but I had to wait a few months to be sentenced. They wanted to know if I'd done it because I was a dedicated Russian spy or just some stupid kid."

I tried to cool him off. "What did this Guido do?" I asked. I felt the pressure relax on the back of my head, but he kept my face against the bars.

"He told me I'd never get out of prison alive. That nobody likes a traitor and the convicts would try to kill me wherever I went. He said my only hope was to escape. Then he told me he was connected to the Mafia and they'd help get me out if I helped *them* when I was on the outside."

"Sounds like the kind of deal the Mafia would make."

He snorted with scorn. "I had nothing to trade – nothing to *give* when I was free."

"So what did you do?"

"I lied. I told them I was a valuable Russian agent and the KGB would pay them well if they got me out. I said I was tremendously valuable because I was one of their top spies."

"He believed you?"

"It wasn't *him* I was trying to convince. It was his bosses.

I wrote all this down on paper and passed it to him. What I *didn't* know was his bosses were the US Government. He passed my notes straight on to them. If they ever doubted I was a spy, they had it now in writing – my *own* writing! They used that against me to get me a 40-year sentence."

"A trap," I said. "That's the way they usually bring you down."

His grip tightened again and he pushed my face so hard into the bars I couldn't see through my left eye. "And now they've sent you to do it again," he hissed.

"No way, Baines!"

"Oh yes. Well it won't work a second time. I won't be caught that way again!"

"Listen, Baines," I said. "I ain't no stoolie. And even if I was, it wouldn't matter if you did tell me what *really* happened. You're *already* in for the full stretch."

He was quiet, so I kept going. "Look. I'm just a simple con... though I can see why you wouldn't believe me. But you've nothing to lose! Whatever happens. You can tell me everything, what difference is it going to make to you. I'm just offering to help you! Straight-up!"

He slowly released the pressure on my head. All he said was, "Yeah." He climbed up back to his bunk, and seemed to fall asleep again.

But 20 minutes later he began to talk.

Chapter Four

"What I didn't know," Baines said in that flat voice of his, "was that the job I had in the mail room was just some kind of test to see if I was reliable. They judged me on my work in those first couple of months. I was just 21 years old when the CIA cleared me for special projects. I was given access to some of the most classified secrets the USA possessed."

"The Birds?" I said.

"The Birds. To be accurate, the correct project name was Rhyolite – the spy satellite system. I was told not to discuss the projects with *anyone*. Not only that, I wasn't permitted to *mention* the Rhyolite codename *or* the fact that the CIA were involved in security."

"Sounds pretty thorough."

He rolled over and looked down at me, amused. "It's one thing to order somebody to keep their mouth shut," he said, "it's another to *check* they're doing what they're supposed to. I was assigned to an underground communications centre called the Dungeon. Hell, my partner, Jerry Hobbs even made a joke of it. He told me the secret codes were worth $20,000 a month to the Russians. Security thorough? Gimme a break!"

"What would the Russians do with the codes?" I asked.

"Not a great deal," he admitted. "The satellites sent messages to the receiver in Australia and the messages were passed on by us to the CIA in America. But they were all in code. What the Russians really needed were the wavelengths that the Rhyolite system was broadcasting on. Only *then* could they use the codes."

"Right. So that's when you decided to make a bit of easy money?"

"No. Not for quite a while. I was being paid badly, but at least I had a job. I was young. I was also pretty impressed by our capabilities."

"Snooping, you mean?"

He frowned. "At first I didn't see spying like that. I saw us as defending the country. Remember, we were afraid that the Russians would launch a nuclear attack on the US at any time. Our satellites would let us see one of their rockets the moment it was launched. We'd have all the warning we needed to retaliate – shoot it down or destroy the launch sites. We could also listen in on military conversations. We could find out about any possible attack hours or even days before it happened."

"So what went wrong?"

"First I discovered we were betraying our friends. In World War II we fought side by side with the Australians in the Pacific. That's why they allowed us to use their country as a secret base. In return they had access to all the information we got from the Rhyolite system."

"Sounds okay," I shrugged.

"Then we sent up the Argus system – this was even more advanced than Rhyolite. Suddenly messages came through telling me not to mention *anything* about Argus to the Australians – not even the name. It was a stab in the back for the Australians." His mouth turned down like he was tasting something sour.

I shrugged. In the world I came from, guys got stabbed in the back all the time.

"It was even worse than that," he went on. "The Australians elected a government that was beginning to ask hard questions about the US receivers in Alice Springs.

Messages came through the Dungeon that made it clear that the CIA went into Australia and started secret operations to stir up trouble for the new government! They wanted to get them voted out before Australia discovered what we were *really* up to on the bases! I got really worked up over that! Who the hell did the CIA think they were? Interfering with the rights of another country... especially those of one of our closest allies."

He lay back and stared at the ceiling.

"Then I discovered they weren't just spying on the Russians," he went on, his voice rising. "They were spying on the French, on the Israelis... More friends!"

I was worried that his loud voice would bring the guards to see what was happening. "Cool it, Baines," I said.

He nodded. There was silence for at least a minute. Then he said. "Ever had a friend, Holtz?"

"Had a dog once."

"Right," he said, ignoring the crack. "A friend's someone you trust. I had a friend like that. We met at school. Flew hawks together. I'd have trusted him with my life."

"He let you down?"

"He changed. Or drugs changed him... And greed. I never cared that much about money. He was different. He was always trying to prove that he was a big shot. His parents had a stack of money, and he'd always had whatever he wanted. Who knows what motivated him? Anyway, when he grew up he was determined to show the world he was somebody important. He started taking drugs in high school. We all did. But then he found you could control people better if you became the drug supplier – the pusher."

"This friend. Was this the Curtis character you mentioned before?"

"Yes."

16

I went to the window and stretched. I could hear the guards opening the cell doors ready to let us out to work. Then I remembered something.

"Hey, Baines," I said, spinning round. "Last night a guy sat opposite us in the canteen. His name was..."

Baines didn't reply. He got down off his bunk and pulled a T-shirt over his head.

"You didn't speak to him," I said.

"No," Baines murmured at last. "I can't forgive him."

"You said he got you bad grades in school. You still blame him for *that*?"

He looked at me fiercely. "I blame him for getting me 40 years inside here."

I wanted to ask 'why?' and 'how?', but held myself in check. "Maybe not 40 years, Baines," I said instead, trying to lighten him up a little. "Not if we can get you out of here."

CHAPTER FIVE

That morning Baines worked in the kitchens while I was allocated to the building and maintenance squad. We didn't see one another till after the midday meal. I changed into trainers and shorts and met him on the track. For a while we jogged in silence. Finally I spoke to him. "You were telling me about Curtis Jonson. I noticed today he's got a black eye."

"Yeah. That'd be Curtis. He could make trouble on the Moon."

"What sort of trouble did he make for you?" I asked.

He didn't answer my question straight away. He seemed to sigh and then, once again, he opened up. "Remember I told you he was a pusher. Well he was making a good living from selling marijuana and cocaine. Then, around the time I was working in the Dungeon, he started dealing in heroin. That's when he started trading in Mexico."

"How did he get the stuff across the border, through customs?"

"All sorts of ways. He used one courier who had a wooden leg. The customs searched the guy every time he crossed the border and never found a thing. The drugs were hidden in the hollow leg!"

"So he never took the risks himself?" I asked as the strain of the run burned my lungs and sweat dripped into my eyes.

"Sure he did. Curtis's trick was to take an aeroplane from Mexico to the US. During the flight he'd hide the drugs behind a panel in the toilet. When the plane landed he left it there and went through customs… completely clean. But he knew the airline schedules backwards. He knew that plane was flying to another US airport later on, so he joined the plane again and took the dope out of the hiding place. When he landed this time he *hadn't* come from a foreign country so he didn't have to go through customs. He just walked out with the dope."

"Neat," I said, half-dead. "Listen. I'll take a break while you do another lap. I'll join you next time you come round."

He waved a hand and set off fast round the track.

I sat on the ground with my back against the inner fence. This was a spot I'd noticed the day before and now I wanted to check it out. They were building a new watchtower further along the fence and today they were starting to fit it with electrics and telephones. I reckoned they'd be moving into it within a week or so.

I shuffled along the ground a little at a time. At last I came to a spot where the old tower blocked my view of the new tower. That meant for a while the guards wouldn't be able to see the spot where I was sitting. Until they pulled the old tower down this was a weak link in the chain that held us in. I took a handkerchief from the waistband of my shorts and carefully tied it to the fence at that spot. Then I sat back and dozed in the Sun while I waited for Baines to complete his circuit.

His face was red and I guess he'd pushed himself hard while he didn't have me holding him back. I stood up stiffly and fell into step with him while he cooled off.

"Did Curtis know about your job?" I asked, picking up the conversation as if I hadn't missed a lap.

"Yeah. I told him."

"What?" I cried. "I thought you weren't supposed to tell anyone! Top secret!"

"He was my friend," Baines said simply. "And when you

19

went to one of Curtis's parties you had so much drink and dope inside you, your mouth ran away with you. That was a weakness of the CIA's work, you see? They never checked out who my friends were. Never knew what I did outside of work. They just told me not to talk about it and they *trusted* me. Crazy!"

"What did Curtis think about your work?"

He shrugged. "Not much at first. He didn't believe the CIA would trust somebody as young as me with the really big secrets. It was only the mention of the money that grabbed his attention."

We walked on round the track. "It was my idea though," Baines said suddenly, "to sell the secrets to the Russians."

"For the money?"

"No, not really," he said quickly. He stopped and looked around the compound, the grey prison complex, the fences. Then he looked at me real sharp.

"Look. If you are from the CIA, sent to spy on me, I'm telling you the truth. I never wanted to hurt the USA. I just wanted to make some kind of *protest*. I wanted to hit out at the government... I didn't want to help the Russians. Does that make sense to you?"

"Get real," I said bluntly. "What exactly *did* you do?"

His chest was heaving as much from the strength of his feelings as from running in the sun. He looked away.

"I told Curtis what my work colleague Jerry Hobbs said about the codes being worth $20,000 a month. I knew I'd have trouble getting out of the country myself to sell them, so I asked him if he'd take some to the Russian Embassy next time he went down to Mexico."

I wiped sweat from my eyes and turned to walk back to the gym block to take a shower.

"Like the way he used a drug runner with a hollow leg,

huh? You used him as a secrets runner?" I suggested.

"Right. I offered to split the money with him right down the middle."

"And he agreed?"

Baines shook his head. "Not at first. He thought I was crazy."

"So you did it yourself?"

"No. Curtis did it in the end. Something happened to change his mind."

We were walking in the cool shadow of the gym block now.

"What happened?" I asked.

"He got himself arrested," he said.

Chapter Six

It seemed Jonson had been arrested before. He was out on probation and knew when he was arrested this time he'd be put away for a long stretch. Baines told me that Jonson would have done anything to stay out of jail – cheat, lie or spy.

The lying came when the arresting officer said Jonson could go free if he paid $15,000 in bail. But Jonson didn't have that sort of money to hand. He was owed $20,000 by other dealers, but he couldn't collect while he was under arrest. That's when he came up with a desperate plan.

"He promised to work for the cops," Baines explained.

"A snitch, eh?" I asked. 'Snitch' was the filthiest word in prison language. Baines and I had both seen what happened to snitches in here. One was being escorted across the exercise yard by two guards when another con lunged at him with a home-made knife. The guard caught the man's arm and took the knife in his own thigh. The attacker got an extra sentence... But he was a hero as far as the rest of the inmates were concerned.

That snitch was one of the lucky ones. He lived. One of the unlucky ones had died right outside our cell door. You just *didn't* snitch. I decided I didn't like this Curtis Jonson.

In the gym we stepped into the cold trickle of water that passed for a shower.

"Of course," Baines went on, "Curtis promised to betray all his drug connections. The police lowered the bail to just $500, and he went free. But he knew the drug people would be after him. He decided all he could do was go on the run. Back to Mexico where he had contacts."

"But he had no income, right?" I said. "He had to take up your offer of selling secrets to the Russians."

"Right. I gave him some code cards from the Dungeon. They were supposed to be shredded when they were finished with, but I'd taken them out in a brief case. Security in there was a joke."

"So where d'you start looking for a Russian spy to sell secrets to?" I wondered.

"I told Curtis to go to the Russian Embassy in Mexico City. I told him to hand over the cards with a note. I wrote something like, 'These are computer cards from a National Security Agency code system. If you want to do business, advise the messenger.' I also told Curtis not to mention my name – ever. Once they knew my name, my life was at risk. However, Curtis knew that if they did get to know my name, they could deal *without* him. I thought my secrecy was guaranteed."

I thought it through. "So you sold *our* secrets to the Russians?"

He stared at the floor.

"No great secrets," he said. "Just code cards that were out of date. They were useless. Just bait. Just part of a scam. Like I said. I was protesting – and yes, we made some money."

It sounded as though he was trying to prove it to himself as much as me. Still, I encouraged his little make-believe.

"And one of the reasons was also to help Jonson?"

"Yeah. To help Curtis. He needed the money. He had drug dealers *and* the cops after him."

"You did all that for a drug-pushing, snitching, greedy little rat. Real tough you got 40 years just for 'trying to help a friend'," I said, spooning it on. But he wasn't fazed.

"Yeah, it is tough," he said simply. There was a pause.

"Well, I guess I'll still try and help you break out," I said at last. He smiled.

"Any ideas?"

I was out of the shower, trying to dry myself off with a prison towel the size of a napkin.

"I need a little more time to work on it," I said. "But I've got something like a plan on my mind."

I dressed quickly and went to the recreation room while Baines went back to his work in the kitchens. There was someone I wanted to meet. I walked right up to the figure huddled in the corner out of the way of the other cons who were shooting pool or playing a hand of cards. His right eye was swollen. It was a red-purple colour and he could hardly open it. A cigarette hung from the corner of his mouth. He looked up suspiciously through a thick, dark fringe.

"Well?" he snarled.

"Curtis Jonson?"

"Who wants to know?"

"Larry. Larry Holtz," I said, smiling like a toothpaste ad and holding out my hand. He ignored it.

"What d'you want?" he said.

"I'm sharing a cell with Mike Baines," I said.

"So?"

"So… I was just interested in the way he says you got him in here."

This time I got a reaction. He snatched the cigarette from his mouth and pointed it at me.

"You got it all wrong, man. *He* got *me* in here."

I decided to play along with this. I sat down next to him and said quietly, "You know, I thought so. His story about him risking his life just to help a friend… Hell, that didn't make sense."

"His life was never at risk!" Jonson snorted. "*I* took all the risks. *I* was the one who went into the Russian Embassy."

"But he was the one that was really spying against the US. He was the one facing the death sentence."

Jonson's lips trembled with anger.

"Listen, Holtz," he said. "Mike Baines was *never* a spy for the Russians."

"But that's what he's in here for!"

"Sure. But Mike was really a spy for the USA. He was planted by the CIA to supply the Russians with all the false information they could use."

"Get out of here!" I said. "If Baines is a CIA agent, how come they've got him locked in here?"

Jonson looked at me real sly, like he was sitting on top of the biggest heap of secrets in the world. His mouth twisted up in a weaselly little grin.

"That's all part of the deal, man," he said, pointing that cigarette at me again. "You just wait and see. They'll find some way to get that guy out of here within a year at the most."

CHAPTER SEVEN

It was easier to get Jonson to talk than it was Baines. I just had to keep needling him. I'd hint that I didn't believe his story, and he'd start leaking information. It just poured right out of him.

"Look, Jonson," I said, "Baines told me you just walked into the Russian Embassy and handed over the code cards. Surely it wasn't that easy!"

"It was," he snapped back.

"So where was the danger for you?"

"The danger was in the fact that the CIA in Mexico would have been watching that Embassy. It was my face they were going to snap on their cameras when they saw me walking in."

"Well I know the CIA's mighty powerful," I said, "but they can't take a picture of every person that walks into the Russian Embassy in Mexico."

"No?" he said. "Who shot President Kennedy?"

"Why... Lee Harvey Oswald."

"And Lee Harvey Oswald was set up by the Russians. The CIA know that because they have a picture of Oswald walking into the Russian Embassy in Mexico. It's a well known fact."

I gave a low whistle. "I see what you mean. You were taking a *lot* of risks."

"You'd better believe it," Jonson said. "But I wasn't too worried about the CIA spotting me. After all, Mike told me we were working for the American government... Except that any money we made from the Russians we could keep!"

"So what happened?" I asked.

"My first contact was a KGB agent called Klimov. He was *real* interested in the codes. But of course the codes were no use without the transmission frequencies."

That tied in with what Baines told me. "So he wouldn't pay you for the codes without the frequencies," I said.

The little guy leaned back against the flaking paint on the concrete wall. "Hey! I'm a business man. One of the best. He paid me because I promised to get him those frequencies. Every time I visited I delivered code sheets and promised the frequencies *next time round*. It was always the next time."

"And if they ever found you were ripping them off, then they'd have killed you," I said.

"Exactly. That's why I reckoned I deserved a bigger share of the money we made."

"I see. You took more of the Russian money than Baines."

"Right."

"And didn't Baines mind?"

Jonson got shifty. Then he said, "He didn't know."

Some friend, I thought. "Surely you didn't stall them for two years with promises of the frequencies?" I asked. He looked at me sharply. "Baines told me you were running this Russian scam for two years."

"We *diversified* a little," he said at last. "The Russians told us to buy these miniature Minolta cameras and photograph documents in the Dungeon. They also wanted photos of the spy satellites themselves. I even went over to Vienna to be trained in using the cameras! I was the *real* secret agent... I left tape fixed to certain lampposts in Mexico City as a signal that I wanted to see Klimov. We had passwords when we met. He had to say, 'Do you know a restaurant in San Francisco?' and I had to reply, 'No, but I know a good one in LA.' My code name was 'Jones' and I

27

had to call Klimov 'Luis'. James Bond is fiction... I was doing this for real, man!"

He sounded more like Groucho Marx than James Bond, but I kept up my very-impressed look.

"And what sort of documents did you photograph?" I asked.

"Anything and everything," he shrugged. "We didn't care. So long as we got paid. Five – ten – twenty thousand dollars a time."

"You must have been worth a fortune," I said.

"Yeah, well, a fortune's no good when you're stuck in Mexico. But I had a passport in another name and I could cross back into the USA whenever I wanted to. I started to double my money – treble it even. I was buying drugs with my Russian money then selling them at a profit in LA."

"Sounds like the perfect scam," I said. "Sell US secrets and make a million."

"With the CIA's approval," Jonson put in quickly. "Don't forget that."

"You sure have some great stories," I said, patting him on the shoulder. "You'll have to tell me some more some time. Got to get back to work now."

"Any time, pal," he said, with his twisted little smile. "Any time."

I walked off to meet my work team and spent the afternoon digging a drainage ditch. As I dug, I went over the idea I had to get Baines out. I decided not to tell him about it until I was sure it could work.

"Ever try to escape when you were on Stone Island?" I asked him the next time I saw him.

"Once," he replied. "We worked our way through a concrete wall to the outside. Trouble was, the hole came out twelve storeys above the street. I've always been a good climber. I spent hours scaling cliffs to get to birds' nests. I'd have made it down, only one of the other cons knew he'd never get out, so he snitched on us..."

"Shame," I said.

Mike gave me a fierce stare. "The thing I learned about escape plans is that the more people there are involved, the more chance there is of being betrayed."

"Right," I muttered.

"So, if your plan is given to the guards, I'll know who the snitch is, won't I?"

"Why would I want to snitch on my own plan! What would be in it for me?"

"Remission. A comfortable life for the rest of your time behind bars," he said.

"No, Baines," I said. "Like I told you, I only have three months to go. Besides, if I snitched and the other cons got to know about it...Well, it wouldn't be too pretty. Just trust me."

"I made that mistake before," he said bitterly.

"I'm not Jonson," I replied, slapping his arm. "Come on. Recreation time. Let's go see the movie."

"What's on?" he asked, relaxing a little.

"Something with Clint Eastwood," I grinned. "*Escape from Alcatraz.*"

Chapter Eight

It may seem weird for prison authorities to show a film about the true story of a prison escape, but that's just what they did. While the rest of the prisoners enjoyed the adventure and cheered for Clint, Baines and I watched and learned.

In the movie, the con played by Eastwood makes a dummy head in the prison workshop. He leaves it in his bunk at night when he's away working on his escape route, so the guards are fooled into thinking he's asleep. When he finally breaks out, the dummy gives him some time on the road – a 'head' start you could say.

Baines must have read my thoughts because when we left the cinema and headed back to our cell, he said, "I liked that idea of leaving a dummy head in the bed. It'd give you a good six hours before they even began to search."

"Yeah, but have you thought about how you'll get through the wire?" I asked.

"That is the million dollar question. I guess a tunnel under the fences would take too long. Try to cut through the wire and you'd be shot. I guess I could hire a helicopter," he said laughing.

"The KGB would give you the money for that, I'll bet!" I joked.

Baines turned on me furiously and I thought for a moment he was going to ram me up against the cell bars again. "I am *not* an employee of the KGB," he shouted. "They have no interest in me now I'm in here."

I held up a hand. "Sure, Baines, I believe you! What I

meant to say was they may help to spring you in gratitude for what you did for them."

"The KGB don't work like that. Once you've lost your usefulness they drop you."

"Is that what happened to you?" I asked as he climbed up onto his bunk bed.

"Well, I certainly wasn't giving them all they wanted," he admitted. "I gave them the codes, but not the transmission frequencies. Curtis kept promising, but the truth was those frequencies were nothing to do with me. They were held by the CIA and there was no way I could get to them… ever. Of course we never admitted that. I passed on reports that the CIA had on Russian submarines. All it told the Russians was that the US was spying on their secret weapons. But they already knew that!"

"But you didn't just do it for the money?"

He shook his head. "No, there was more to it than that. I thought we'd gone too far – as a country I mean. We were hurting our friends. And yes, there was the excitement, I guess. The fear of getting caught sends your blood racing. That fear is like a drug. Twice I was nearly caught in 1976 and, d'you know, I enjoyed it!"

"What happened?"

"The first time, my colleague in the Dungeon, Jerry Hobbs, announced we were having an inspection by a new security chief and he was on his way. I was worried about the code cards I'd been photographing. They were kept in sealed envelopes until they were needed, and I'd been breaking those seals to photograph them. I'd even put some back upside down!"

"And the security guy spotted the broken seals?" I asked.

Baines shook his head in wonder. "If he did, he said nothing. He passed right over them."

"Why do you think that was?"

"Either because the CIA are so bad at security he didn't know his job, or else they were so *good* that they knew exactly what was going on. They let me get on with it because they were planting useless information. What the CIA calls *disinformation*."

"You think you were set up by the CIA?"

"It's possible," he said.

"That's what Jonson believes, isn't it?"

Mike looked at me suspiciously. "You've talked to him?"

"I bumped into him in the recreation room," I admitted.

"There was a time when I wanted to kill him," Baines said.

"Because he got you in here?"

"No. Because almost from the beginning he was pressuring me to get more and more secrets for the Russians and I knew he was taking *more* than half the money. When I tried to get out of the stealing secrets racket he threatened to blackmail my father with what he knew about my spying. He even had copies of all the documents I'd taken from the Dungeon. After a year I wanted out of our partnership. I wanted direct contact with the Russians. I even bought a gun..."

"And?"

"I planned to take Curtis out to the desert to fly the hawks. When we were alone out there I'd decided to put a couple of bullets in him. But I couldn't go through with it. We'd been kids together."

He was lost in his own thoughts for a few minutes. Then he said, "I finally met the Russians. In Mexico. I told them I couldn't get the frequencies they wanted. That's when they realized Curtis had been lying to them. I thought maybe they'd kill him and I'd be free."

"They didn't. Obviously."

"No. They still wanted more, just the way Curtis had wanted more. I decided I'd give them one last delivery. A big one. One that would make me enough money to leave my job, go back to college and fly hawks. I had access to a top secret document called the Pyramider file."

"I thought you said you never gave them anything useful, Baines," I said.

"I thought I hadn't," he replied, covering his face with his hands.

CHAPTER NINE

Baines said nothing more that night, but next morning I asked him straight out whether he'd known the Pyramider Project was valuable when he sold it to the Russians.

"I knew it was top secret, but *useless*," he said. "By the time I passed it on to the Russians, the Pyramider Project had already been shelved. The Russians could read all about a top secret spy system that the US planned. But the Russians wouldn't know that we couldn't afford it!"

I thought about this for a moment. It was plain to me I didn't know what was on the level and what wasn't. But there was something about Baines. Whatever happened, I was still going to help him break out.

On my suggestion, we skipped the run round the fencing and went to the craft workshop. There wasn't anyone around so we began to make a dummy head. We blew up a balloon and began to build up layers of gummed paper around it. It wasn't going to be a masterpiece, or even look like Baines, but in the dark laid on the top bunk with blankets up around it, I thought it would fool the guards.

"So what *is* your plan to get me out?" he asked quietly as we worked on the head.

"I've still got some details to sort out," I said. "I need to have another look at a weakness I've spotted in the perimeter fence first. When I've done that I'll tell you all about it."

I have to give Baines this, he was real patient. He just nodded and went on working on the head.

"So what *was* so secret about the Pyramider Project you tried to sell to the Russians?" I asked him.

"It was a satellite system like Rhyolite or Argus but it wasn't there to take pictures. It was there to act like some telephone exchange in the sky. It allowed the CIA to talk to their agents any time, wherever they were in the world. The messages would be automatically protected by codes. Spies in foreign countries could send instant reports back home with no risk to themselves. But it would only work if the Russians knew nothing about it."

"Then you told them."

"I did pass on the plan for Pyramider. What I didn't pass on was that the government had refused to give the CIA the money to build the system. That made Pyramider so *un*-secret that the file wasn't even locked away in the safe. It was out in the open for me to take home and photograph."

"So was that when you got caught?"

"That was when *Curtis* got caught," he said. "Now the Russians had found out he was a liar, they didn't want to know him. He used all his secret marks on lampposts, but they never turned up for a meeting. In the end he grew desperate and tried to throw a message over the wall into the Embassy. Mexican police spotted him and wanted to know what he was up to. They even suspected he was the man who'd murdered a Mexican policeman a month before. They took him in and tried to beat a confession out of him."

"But he was innocent," I said.

"He was innocent of the Mexican cop's murder. Trouble was, they searched his hotel room for evidence and found the photographs of the Pyramider file we were trying to sell. They informed the CIA and the whole story came out."

"Bad luck," I muttered.

"Not *luck*," Baines said. "It was simple stupidity on Curtis's part. He was so doped on heroin by that time he didn't know what he was doing."

"Didn't you have time to run?"

"Where to?" he shrugged. "I knew they would be watching all the airports. If I tried to leave the country it would be a sure sign that I was guilty. No, I just went back to the desert, hawking. I went with a friend, Jack Prince. We spent two days trying to trap young hawks."

He gave a harsh laugh.

"What I should have guessed was there was a trap waiting for *me*! We got back to the cabin and a car came skidding down the hill to block our path. They must have had the shack staked-out while we were up in the hills. When I stepped out of the station wagon I saw gun barrels trained on me from every direction. I knew the CIA get excitable – trigger-happy. One wrong move and I was dead."

It was quiet in the cell. Baines shivered. "It wasn't just the guns. It was the hatred. 'Traitor' they called me. Over and over again. 'Traitor'. It never hit me till then what I'd done. They called me traitor like it was the dirtiest word on Earth."

"It's not as if you killed somebody," I said.

"Yeah," he said, "but I found out what a traitor was soon enough. Betraying your country is bad – I know that. But betraying a friend, well, to me it's worse."

"That's what Curtis Jonson did to you?"

Baines nodded. "My lawyers told me that his defence was that I'd told him he wasn't betraying his country. He said I told him we were working for the CIA – giving the Russians false information. He said he thought he was working for his country – if we were passing on real secrets, then I'd lied to him. He said that *I* was the traitor and *he* was the innocent sucker."

"That's pretty rough, Baines. I can see why you hate him."

"Not only that, but when we were sentenced he got 20

years, I got 40. Obviously the judge believed I was worse than him. The CIA experts told him we were not working for the government and that selling Pyramider would have put everyone in the USA at risk. With the CIA and Curtis against me, I was lucky I only got 40 years!"

I smoothed another piece of paper on the dummy head, over the lump that was becoming a nose.

"Forty or 140 years," I said, "it doesn't matter now. We're going to get you out of here."

CHAPTER TEN

We left the dummy head to dry and went back to work. The next day I decided to let Baines in on the escape plan. We went out jogging around the perimeter fence, and I slowed down when I reached the spot I'd marked.

"Stop right there, Baines," I said. "Look at that new guard tower."

"I can't. It's hidden by the old one," he replied.

"Exactly. This is the one place where you'll have a good chance of escaping over the wire."

He looked at me, and smiled.

"Not bad," he said.

"Let's go before someone sees us."

We jogged on till we were well away from the spot.

"I'd have to go after dark," he said.

"Yeah. Trouble is, they won't allow prisoners into that area after we return to our cells at 4 pm. We'll have to get you there during the day and hide you. When it gets dark you can come out of hiding and climb the fence."

"I'll be missed in the kitchen."

"I've thought about that. It'd be better if you got transferred out of the kitchens and into my work squad. I won't report you missing till you're well away," I said.

"Fine. So how do I hide on a bare patch of dirt with no cover for 80 metres?"

"You hide *under* the dirt," I told him. "We go out to the fence to repair a blocked drain. We dig a hole in the ground, you slip down in the hole and stay there till nightfall."

He ran on without a word, thinking of all the objections he could.

"But there isn't a blocked drain there," he said finally.

"So? We'll just have to *invent* one. Whoa! Let's take a break!" In his excitement, Baines had been forcing the pace and my legs were turning to mush.

I sank to the ground and rested my back against the fence. Guards watched us from the nearest tower. One reached for a microphone and the loudspeakers crackled, "Move away from the fence!"

I got up stiffly and tottered to a spot ten metres away and dropped back down. Baines stood over me.

"How do you invent a blocked drain where it doesn't exist?" he asked.

"Listen. Each day we have a work timetable from the senior prison officer in charge of our group. We'll just forge the instruction so it says we have to dig a trench at that spot."

"And how long have you been a forger?" he asked.

"I'm not," I shrugged. "But some of the guys in the next block can do it. It'll cost you a pack of 20 cigarettes."

"I don't like the idea of other cons being involved. I've told you. The more people that know about it, the more chance there is of being snitched on."

"Okay, okay! Maybe so. But you do have to trust someone sooner or later. You trust me, right?"

"I don't trust *anyone*. If you're a plant by the CIA, then you'll get me out because the CIA want me out. If you're not, then I really don't get why you're helping me. Okay, so you think there's some cash in it for you, or some help on the outside. Well maybe there is, maybe there ain't. I don't see how you can trust *me*. Whatever – I can't afford to trust you."

"Baines," I said, reaching out and gripping his arm hard. "It's true I don't know if there's really much in it for me.

And it's not as if we made some kind of a deal. But let's just say I don't like to see a good guy rot in this hole. So maybe you don't believe me. Way I see it, neither of us have a thing to lose by trusting each other."

"Keep moving! Keep moving!" the loudspeaker crackled. I got to my feet and we continued our jog.

"Okay, Holtz," Baines said at last. "I guess maybe you've got a point. But still. The less people know about my escape, the better chance I have of succeeding."

"I agree. But the little forger who's going to make the work pass is going to have to be told what's going on. It's just a risk we're going to have to take."

He sighed. "I guess so."

"And another thing," I said. "The other two cons in the digging detail are going to find out... "

"But I *trust* them," I added with a smile.

CHAPTER ELEVEN

On the morning of January 21, 1980, Mike Baines was ready to break out of Lompoc. Neither of us had slept much and we got up around 5 am.

The dummy head, which we'd finished a few days previously, was hidden under my bunk. If the guards chose to search our cell during the day – well, we'd had it.

At 8 am we went down to breakfast. Baines ate extra, packing up on food because he wasn't too sure when he'd see his next meal.

At 8.30 am we headed back to our cell ready to change into work clothes. Baines stopped by the pay phones. "You go ahead," he said. A few minutes later he came back to the cell, we changed and walked down to the main door of the block.

"You got friends waiting outside?" I asked.

"What?" he snapped back nervously.

"The phone call…"

"You don't want to know," he said.

"Fine," I muttered. "I'm risking an extra year in this place if I'm caught helping… And you say it's none of my business."

But Baines didn't look at me. He carried right on walking.

We met the other two members of the work party, collected digging tools and headed towards the gate into the inner fence. "Pass for four maintenance crew to repair a drain," I said to the guard. I stole a look at Baines. The sweat was just standing on his brow. He looked at me – and dropped the shovel he was holding.

"Pick it up," the guard barked, kicking it towards him.

Baines stooped, breathing heavily, and took such a firm grip of the shaft I thought he was going to take a swing at the guard. The man in uniform stepped back a pace, and his hand dropped to the butt of his pistol. For a few seconds the two stared at one another. Then Baines dropped his eyes and lowered the shovel.

After this little drama, the guard scarcely glanced at our forged work pass.

"Have a nice day," he said with a mean smile as we walked through the gate. "Going to be mighty hot digging out there."

He was right. It was like working in a furnace, and the dirt next to the old tower was packed hard. We dug in pairs, one using a pick while the other shovelled.

At noon we stopped for water and sandwiches. I'd already told the other two cons that Baines was going to make a break for it, but I hadn't told them how. This seemed like a good moment.

"We finish digging at 2.50 pm and collect planks from the wood store," I said. "We board over the trench and say we're waiting for the new drain pipe to be delivered. At 3.00 pm the guards change. Baines climbs down into the trench and we cover him with boards. The old guards saw four men working here. The new guards will see three. Nothing strange about that. At 3.30 pm we return to the cell block and Baines stays here till dark. Get it?"

They nodded. They weren't the kind to ask questions.

The trench grew longer and deeper as the afternoon wore on. At 2.50 pm I went for the planks with Baines. When we returned, we worked fast to cover up the trench.

At 3.00 pm, the cons we'd posted as lookout told us the new guards had arrived at the tower. "Time to get in my grave," said Baines. He wasn't too far wrong: it was going to be dark and hot as hell in there, though Baines could breathe through gaps in the planking.

He slipped down into the trench. When he was settled, I passed down a pair of wire-clippers I'd stolen from the workshop and carried out here stuck in my waistband. Baines would need those to cut his way through the wire netting. I also gave him a toothbrush thick with grease. The grease could be smeared on the alarm wires wound around sections of the fence, making them less sensitive to vibrations as Baines clipped away.

We moved the last plank over him. It was time to get going. "Good luck, bud," I said.

"Look me up when you get out," he replied from his hideout.

"Sure," I said. "Put the champagne on ice."

I tested the planking with my foot. Underneath, lying in the dirt, darkness and heat, was America's most dangerous spy. It was pretty hard to believe.

I turned away without another word. My part in the escape wasn't over yet, and a lot of things could still go wrong. As we entered the cell block, I handed over the second forged work pass – the one that said there'd been three of us out there in the sun. The guard at the gate thought he was some kind of a comedian.

"You guys been digging a tunnel to get out?" he grinned.

"Would we dig one to get *in*?" I said. The smile slid off his face. He thrust the pass back in my hand.

When I got back to the cell I fumbled under my bunk for the dummy head. At first I couldn't find it. My heart pounded. Then I felt the hair. Baines had cut off tufts of his own to stick on the dummy as a realistic touch.

I buried the head deep in Baines's pillow, turning it to face the wall. Then I put my own pillow and a rolled-up blanket in his bunk to make the outline of a body.

An hour later, the guard stuck his head round the door and looked above me. "What's his problem?" he asked.

"Been working out in the sun all day," I replied.

"I guess life in the kitchen turned the traitor soft," he said before he slammed the door shut.

But Baines wasn't soft at all. Some time that night he managed to break out of there to freedom.

CHAPTER TWELVE

I never saw or heard from Mike Baines again. However, as far I was concerned that wasn't the end of the story.

The guards discovered our little trick with the dummy head the next morning when we were due for breakfast. You should have seen their faces! They began squawking at me like a bunch of hens in a coop. Of course they interrogated me, asking a lot of dumb questions about how and when and where. But I wasn't going to make it any easier for them. I clammed right up.

After about an hour they found the holes Baines had cut in the wire fencing. I was led to the governor's office and told to stand outside his door while he talked to some government agents inside.

I stared at the floor and knew my parole, due in three months, would be cancelled. Suddenly I was aware of a small, unkempt figure, sidling up and staring at me with little red rat's eyes. It was Curtis Jonson.

"The CIA sent you, didn't they?" he said.

"What are you talking about?"

"The CIA. Mike Baines was working for the CIA. They had that mock trial and sentenced him to 40 years so the Russians would believe he was a genuine spy. But he was working for the CIA all along, wasn't he?" Jonson clutched at my sleeve.

"You're crazy."

"But they promised they'd let him escape. The CIA planted you in here to help him, didn't they? And so it's my turn next," he babbled.

"What're you talking about?"

"I was spying for the CIA, *wasn't* I? They can't keep me locked up in here now, can they? Now they'll let *me* go. I was working for America too!"

"You were working for the money," I said. "You're a heroin dealer, a liar and a creep. I hope you rot in this hole, Jonson. Now take your hand off me, or I'll break every finger on it."

He backed away, looking hurt and confused. For a moment I thought he was going to burst into tears.

"You're not CIA?" he whimpered. Then his face brightened again. "Hey, then you must be KGB! The Russians put you in here to get him out. Hey, comrade! I'm one of you! I helped you!"

A guard dragged Jonson away.

The door to the office opened and I stepped inside. The prison governor sat behind his desk, and standing next to him was a big guy in a dark suit. He had close-cropped silvery hair, steel-rimmed glasses and he was from the CIA, sure as if he had the letters tattooed across his forehead.

"So the Hawk flew the nest, Mr Holtz?" the agent said, smiling.

"If you mean Baines escaped, yeah."

"And what did you hope to gain by helping him?"

"Don't know. Maybe I just liked the guy."

He sighed.

"Well, you were due for parole in three months," he said. "Now the governor here tells me you'll get an extra 18 months."

"I guessed that might happen," I said.

"Of course," he added, "strictly speaking, we should give you an extra couple of years for abetting an escape."

I didn't reply. I just let him say what he had to say.

"My advice to you is that you co-operate with our

enquiries. CIA agents will question you over the next week. Tell them everything you know. Including how you helped Baines break out of here."

"Can I ask *you* a question?" I said when he'd finally finished.

"Sure."

"All the time Baines was passing secrets to the Russians – were you guys just using him? I mean, was he just a 'plant' so you could feed the communists false information?"

"That's two questions," he replied with that smile of his. There was a silence.

"Listen, Mr Holtz," he said then. "Officially, our view is that Mike Baines betrayed his country."

"What about unofficially then?"

He didn't reply. He just stood there smiling at me.

Then the governor leaned forward and said. "That'll do, Holtz" – my cue to leave. As I opened the door, I looked back at the man from the CIA. He was still smiling.

GLOSSARY

ARGUS
Satellite system planned in the late 1970s to
replace Rhyolite. Each satellite was to have
an antenna double the size of Rhyolite, vastly
increasing the number and quality of signals.
The system was never built.

CIA
(CENTRAL INTELLIGENCE AGENCY)
US agency set up in the late 1940s to protect
the government from hostile foreign nations.
The CIA employs agents in over 150 countries
to send back information which it then
assesses, offering its analysis to other US
agencies. The CIA also attempts to prevent
any risk to the national security posed by
foreign spies.

DISINFORMATION
False information released to deliberately
mislead people.

THE DUNGEON
The code room of the defence complex where
Baines worked. To reach the room, one had to
pass three checkpoints and a number of
armed guards while one's every move was
followed by close-circuit TV monitors. The

door to the room itself was of thick steel, like those used in bank vaults. Only three people knew the combination number to open it – Baines was one.

FBI
(FEDERAL BUREAU OF INVESTIGATION)
Division of the US Justice Department, run from the national headquarters in Washington DC. The FBI is the most important investigating division of the government. Part of the Bureau deals with law enforcement and looks into federal crimes including kidnapping, espionage and treason. The FBI also gathers information on people or groups that could threaten national security.

GPALS
(Global Protection Against Limited Strikes) President Bush's defence programme for the United States, which was much reduced from the enormous SDI defence strategy of Reagan's government.

KGB
A government agency of the former Soviet Union. The letters KGB are an abbreviation of the words 'Committee for State Security' in Russian. Its main function was to ensure that the Communist Party kept control of the former Soviet Union. It operated a secret police force, and was also involved with

gathering information about other countries and secretly aiding foreign governments or other organizations that it considered sympathetic or friendly. The KGB was disbanded in 1991 when the former Soviet Union was dissolved.

PYRAMIDER

A US spy satellite system developed at the same time as Rhyolite, but expressly designed for communication with CIA agents in foreign cities. The system employed 'frequency-hopping' – signals transmitted on a variety of frequencies so they could be 'hidden' among other radio traffic.

RHYOLITE

A US spy satellite system designed to orbit the Earth and eavesdrop on foreign microwave signals. Each satellite carried a battery of antennae which could monitor Communist radio signals and telephone conversations. Rhyolite satellites were launched in 1973, 1977 and 1978.

SATELLITE

An orbiting spacecraft that can relay radio, telegraph, telephone and television signals. Stations on Earth transmit signals to the satellite, which then conveys these signals to destinations all over the world.

SDI
(STRATEGIC DEFENCE INITIATIVE)

Reagan's planned US defence programme, later nicknamed 'Star Wars'. Announced in the early 1980s, this aggressive programme involved building a defence of satellite gunships as the ultimate deterrent against hostile nations.

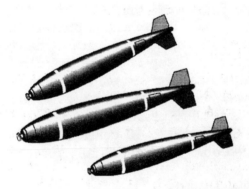

Biographies

This story contains fictional characters involved in a true-life mystery. Before you look at the facts and make up your own mind, here's a brief biography of the characters:

MICHAEL BAINES
(ACTUAL CHARACTER - DISGUISED NAME)

From a wealthy Los Angeles family, son of a former FBI agent. He was the oldest of nine children. Deeply religious as a child, Baines was a highly intelligent boy who enjoyed taking risks. His childhood interest in birds grew into a passion for training hawks. Was offered a good career in the defence company which created top secret, very advanced spy and weapon systems. He chose to sell those secrets to the Russian secret service – the KGB. Sentenced to 40 years in prison, but escaped only to be eventually recaptured.

CURTIS JONSON
(ACTUAL CHARACTER - DISGUISED NAME)

Adopted son of a wealthy Los Angeles doctor. A friend of Mike Baines at school, he later shared his interest in falconry. Began taking drugs while at school but soon found there was more to be gained by drug-dealing. When he was arrested for dealing, he had to find another easy way to make money. He took the defence secrets from Mike Baines and sold them to the Russians. When he was caught, he claimed he was selling worthless information and the American CIA knew all about it. Sentenced to 20 years in prison.

LARRY HOLTZ
(ACTUAL CHARACTER - DISGUISED NAME)
A prisoner in Lompoc prison at the same time as Curtis Jonson and Mike Baines, convicted on bank robbery charges. After assisting Baines's escape he was transferred to a federal prison near Oklahoma City. He had just three months of his sentence left to serve when he helped Baines escape. Instead he was sentenced to a further 18 months. His reasons for helping Baines remain somewhat obscure. Was he motivated by a sincere desire to help his cellmate or was there a more sinister explanation?

KLIMOV, KNOWN AS 'LUIS'
(ACTUAL CHARACTER - DISGUISED NAME)
A KGB agent, Klimov was the first to meet Jonson in Mexico City. He gave the American tens of thousands of dollars for the secrets Baines was stealing, clearly believing they were valuable. However, Klimov eventually cut off Jonson's flow of cash. Had he simply lost his faith in Jonson the drug dealer, or discovered that the 'secrets' were worthless?

Classified Files

Who was telling the truth? The CIA when they said Mike Baines was stealing valuable secrets and risking the lives of everyone in the USA? Curtis Jonson, who claimed he always believed they were working for the CIA to give the Russians *false* information? Or Mike Baines when he maintained he was disillusioned with his country, and that he knew he was giving the Russians worthless information anyway?

Above all, what was the *real* reason for Baines's involvement in espionage?

Look at these possibilities, and decide which you think is the most believable. . .

Baines wanted money.
Baines had expensive tastes. He wanted a sports car and he wanted drugs (though he was never an addict like Jonson). He also wanted to go back to college to study the history of falconry. Baines was paid less that $150 a week at the defence corporation and so took a second job, working through the night as a bar tender. Selling secrets could bring him a lot of easy money. The biggest risk was photographing the Pyramider Project papers. However, the papers were so valuable that he aimed to make $50,000 from their sale; then he could

safely 'retire' from spying. Indeed, after photographing Pyramider he resigned from his defence job and, at the time of his arrest, was back at college.

BUT...

Surely if Baines was driven solely by financial pressures to commit treason, he would have been more meticulous about payment? Instead, Jonson sold secrets for $10,000, told Baines the Russians had paid just $5,000, and handed over $3,000.

Baines hated America.

Even though he lived comfortably in the USA, Baines resented the way the US government treated other nations. He believed it used its international might to bully weaker powers, and was particularly critical of America's disastrous involvement in the Vietnam War. He also discovered that the US was deceiving its allies – to the extent, for instance, of meddling with Australian politics. So he simply decided to reduce US military power by selling its secrets to the Soviet Union.

BUT...

There were millions of Americans who were just as innocent as the peasants in Vietnam. They would suffer if the Russians defeated the USA in a war thanks to Baines's betrayal of weapon secrets. In hitting back at his government, Baines was also hitting out at every US man, woman and child.

Baines loved Russia and the Communist system.

Though his father was staunchly anti-Communist, Mike Baines was a rebel who would deliberately turn away from anything his father believed in. Baines wanted to see the Russian system in place in the USA. By gaining access to US military secrets the Russians would become the most powerful nation on Earth; they would know all about US defences and find ways to overcome them in a war. After a Communist victory, Baines would be a hero. He met the Russians after two years of selling secrets to them. They told him to go back to college and find out more about their way of life. In fact, when Baines was arrested he had just begun a course on Russian history.

BUT...

Baines never claimed he wanted the Russians to defeat the US in war. Perhaps he began to learn about Russia simply because he thought he might have to defect at some stage. His partner in espionage, Curtis Jonson, was a staunch anti-Communist, so it seems unlikely that the two friends would work together in espionage if they had such strongly opposing views.

Baines wanted world peace.

He believed the best way to prevent nuclear war was to make sure there was a balance of power between the US and

Russia. Since US spy satellite systems were more advanced than the Russian ones, selling US secrets would help to keep the military might of the two countries 'balanced'.

BUT...

In handing secrets to the Russians, there was a chance the 'balance' would tip *their* way and peace would be destroyed anyway. Also it is unimaginable that one man could affect the balance of power.

Baines enjoyed the thrill of spying. A boyhood friend reported that Baines had always enjoyed taking a risk. Later, however, he found himself in a boring job sitting at a code machine and passing on messages. Everyone in the Dungeon was bored. They smuggled in alcohol though it was against the rules, and held parties. But that wasn't risky enough for Baines. He decided to sell secrets just to see if it could be done. The secret codes weren't very valuable to the Russians – not without details of the transmission frequencies – but the risk of smuggling them out was exciting. Photographing documents seemed dangerous and had all the drama and adventure of being a secret agent. Baines even added to the danger by choosing the most unreliable partner he could find – Curtis Jonson.

BUT...

Baines must have realized that the greatest risk was a war against Russia. If he really believed in peace, then he wouldn't have endangered thousands of lives simply for the sake of his own entertainment.

Baines wanted to help his old friend Jonson.

Jonson was trouble, but Baines and he had been friends for years. When Jonson got into serious difficulties with the police, Baines offered to help him out. The staff in the Dungeon had said their secrets were worth thousands of dollars to the Russians. Baines believed that he could get his friend away from the drugs trade and into something 'safer'. He stole the secrets, passed them on to Jonson and let him make arrangements to be paid by the Russians.

BUT...

When Jonson began to boast about being a spy, he made life a little too dangerous for comfort. Baines could simply have stopped supplying the secrets: he didn't. Instead he sent messages in code inviting the KGB to ditch Jonson as a go-between, and to contact Baines for more secret US information.

Baines wanted to feel important.

Baines had delusions of grandeur. When he was out with his hawks he fantasized that he was an ancient prince. If he stole secrets and sold them to the Russians, he could imagine himself controlling the balance of power on an immense scale.

Russia was desperate for knowledge, and he could give them as much – or as little – as he wanted.

Mike Baines could have stolen the secrets for any one of the above reasons. Or he could have stolen them for a mixture of two or three of them. He may not even have understood why he did it himself.

BUT...

He may not have stolen the secrets at all! This is the explanation given by Curtis Jonson – and one that a number of authorities agree with. According to this explanation:

COULD BAINES ACTUALLY HAVE BEEN A LOYAL AMERICAN WORKING FOR THE CIA?

The Russians knew a little about the Rhyolite spy satellite system, but not much. They could have put a lot of effort into finding the truth by sending in skilled spies or sabotaging important parts of the system. The CIA decided to lay a false trail; to give the KGB information, without a lot of effort – false information or *disinformation*. They found a completely reliable young man in Mike Baines; he was the son of a former FBI agent and was willing to do anything to help his country. He was asked to take a job in the defence corporation and to see what secrets he could sneak out.

When Baines had worked there a while, he was told by the CIA to start passing on some secrets to Curtis Jonson, who would sell them to the Russians in Mexico. Of course the CIA made quite sure that the secret codes had no transmission frequencies to go with them – they were of no real use to the Russians, but they would make sure the KGB trusted Baines and Jonson.

Once the KGB had swallowed the bait, the CIA began using the two friends to give more and more disinformation to the Russians. Finally they would give them a huge project called Pyramider. The Russians would see that the Americans possessed an advanced satellite system and would not dare to start a war.

The Russian military would be paralyzed by the fear of Pyramider – a spy system that didn't exist, never would exist and was in fact only a CIA scare tactic.

But the CIA plan went wrong. Jonson was arrested by the Mexican police when he tried to deliver Pyramider. The CIA told Baines they'd have to abort the spying plan. They wanted the Russians to go on believing that Jonson and Baines were genuine spies, so they arrested the friends and put them on public trial.

"Don't worry, Mike," they said. "You'll be sentenced to 40 years in prison but you'll never have to serve it. Within a year or two we'll make sure you escape. You can have a new identity, plastic surgery to change your appearance... and lots of money to enjoy for the rest of your life."

Baines played his part perfectly. He claimed he hated the US government and had spied for peace. He denied he had been set up by the CIA, and pretended to defend himself at his trial.

The CIA later put Larry Holtz in the cell to help Mike break out. Holtz was a genuine criminal, but he was promised a reward after release if he helped.

BUT...

There is one major flaw in this explanation: why would a man with three months to serve incur a heavier sentence to help a relative stranger escape? He would have known that his part in the escape would be discovered and he'd end up with 18 months!

Holtz didn't do it because he was kind-hearted. Only one explanation makes sense. 'Larry Holtz' was to be well-rewarded for the extra 18 months he'd spend in prison. That is the conspiracy theory explaining the Baines case. Is that how it happened?

TREASON OR DISINFORMATION?

When Mike Baines and Curtis Jonson went
to their separate trials, there were two
matters that were never discussed
satisfactorily:

**a) How sensitive was the information Baines
took from the Dungeon?**

b) How involved was Baines with the CIA?

The questions are linked. If Mike was working
for the CIA, or if he was being 'used' by them,
then the secrets he passed on were worthless.
Some have argued that if they *were*, then he
must have been working for the CIA.

It's worth looking first at the secrets and
making up your own mind as to their value.

The secrets *were* sensitive because...

The messages about CIA activity in Australia
could severely damage US-Australian
relations. In the event, this was what
happened. When the Australians found out –
possibly through a KGB 'leak' – that the CIA
were indeed involved in influencing the
Australian political situation, they felt
betrayed.

The CIA had been gathering top secret information about Russia from their Rhyolite spy satellites. Rhyolite information included the launch sites and performance of Russian missiles, and this could be used to alter US defences. So the Rhyolite signals were priceless. After Baines passed Rhyolite secrets to the Russians, the CIA noticed that the Russians began to communicate *in code*. The US was left in the dark again. Of course, the Russians may have decided to encode all their secret transmissions anyway. There's no proof that the change to codes was a direct result of secrets leaked from the Dungeon.

Spy satellites were such a threat that both the Russians and the Americans were creating weapons to deal with them, such as laser cannons to shoot down opposition spy satellites. The knowledge the Russians had about the Rhyolite satellites would allow them easily to locate and destroy them in the event of a war.

When details of the Argus spy satellites were passed on to the KGB, the Russians could see both what the US had in the skies at that time and what they were planning to put there in the future.

Baines gave the Russians details of US observations on Russian submarine movements, and even details of spy information on China. The CIA wanted to show that Mike Baines had done a lot of harm to the USA. They said some of the secrets were so important they couldn't even reveal them at his trial. They almost let Mike Baines go without a trial – because they didn't want to admit that the US had spy satellites.

The secrets were *not* sensitive because...

The Pyramider Project file was casually left out of the safe. There is a possibility that it was left out *deliberately* – a bait to trap the spy who called himself the Hawk.

Pyramider was a project that used advanced electronics to communicate with spies. But there was nothing 'secret' about these. Any electronics engineer would know about it. As Baines's defence council argued in court, "We have evidence that the government could have gone to any Radio Shack to get that kind of thing."

Pyramider was too expensive to build and run. The CIA realized it would not get money from the US government to build it. They abandoned the idea in late 1973, and the Pyramider file was locked away for *three years* before Baines was employed in the Dungeon.

The code cards were worthless without transmission frequencies. Baines always argued that he knew that. He promised the Russians he would obtain those frequencies; he never did, and he knew he never could. Selling the code cards was just a way of making easy money and quite harmless to the USA.

It is likely that, using their own radar systems, the Russians had spotted the Rhyolite spy satellites anyway.

No one can agree on the value of the secrets that were lost through Baines. If you believe the information was worthless, then you may also believe the CIA allowed Mike Baines to pass it on to the Russians. You then have to decide what evidence there is to prove his involvement with the CIA. Again there are arguments on both sides. Try to decide for yourself.

Mike Baines *must* have been working for the CIA because...

Curtis Jonson claimed that Baines was. Jonson met Baines after their arrests. He knew him better than anyone and expected his old friend to be worried about being caught; after all, they faced a possible death sentence. However, Jonson was amazed at Baines's casual attitude. Baines seemed to believe he would get off scot-free.

Jonson visited the Russian Embassy in Mexico City at least three times. The US secret services photographed all visitors and investigated them. They must have had pictures of Jonson – yet for some reason they did nothing about his illegal activities.

Mike Baines came from a good family, but he himself was not particularly stable. His best friend was a convicted drugs dealer; he had dropped out of college to become a low-paid clerk. As Jonson put it: **It doesn't make sense that an alcoholic [himself] and a pot head [Mike] could do this on their own. The CIA would surely *not* allow a person like Mike to view such secret information. Not unless they *wanted* to use him to spread false information to the Russians.**

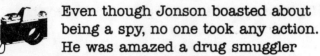 Even though Jonson boasted about being a spy, no one took any action. He was amazed a drug smuggler such as himself could cross into Mexico so easily, time after time, without being arrested. He argued that this proved the CIA were making it easy for him.

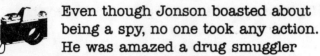 Lompoc prison was a high security prison. Escape for America's most notorious spy should have been impossible. Baines managed it, but he must have had some outside help. Was it from the CIA?

Mike Baines was *not* working for the CIA because...

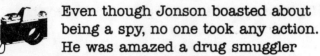 Mike Baines never claimed he was working for the CIA. Of course, that could have been part of a deal worked out between them.

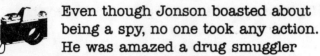 The CIA would not allow him to use a criminal like Curtis Jonson as a go-between. He was not the sort of person they could trust if they were planning a campaign of disinformation.

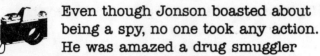 The CIA didn't know why Baines had betrayed America, even after the trial. That's why they put a 'snitch' in the cell next to him – the man

called 'Guido' in the story. They wanted to find out the whole truth from Baines. Would they have used 'Guido' to obtain this information if Baines was in fact one of their own agents?

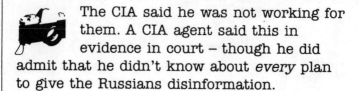 The CIA said he was not working for them. A CIA agent said this in evidence in court – though he did admit that he didn't know about *every* plan to give the Russians disinformation.

The CIA were shocked by the weak security at the defence company and in the Dungeon. After Baines's trial, they tightened up security at all secret defence establishments. If Baines had truly been a security 'success' – a CIA 'plant' who had confused the Russians – then they would not have worried about it.

Of course, there is a further – very credible – possibility: Mike Baines could have been working for the CIA *without knowing it*.

As Baines said, it is strange that two amateurs such as he and Jonson should be able to get away with so much. Perhaps the CIA had spotted their sale of secrets and begun to leave false or worthless secrets for Baines to pass to the Russians. The CIA could of course never admit this ruse in court, which would conclude that the two spies had been illegally 'entrapped' (forced to

incriminate themselves). If that is indeed
what happened, then the CIA used Baines
and Jonson as unsuspecting channels of
disinformation.

Baines saw himself as the Hawk. Perhaps
the CIA saw him instead as the Pigeon.

Spy Systems

The Rhyolite spy satellite system was hovering over the world sending information back to ground receivers in Australia. That information was then passed through Baines in the Dungeon to the CIA.

Rhyolite was top secret, but the Russians must have known these electronic eyes in space were watching them. They couldn't disrupt the system, and they couldn't read the information. Even though Baines gave them the codes, they never discovered what frequency the electronic messages were being broadcast on.

But Pyramider was different. It was a spy communications network that the Russians almost certainly knew nothing about. In fact, they never received details of the Pyramider Project; Curtis Jonson was on his way to deliver it when he was arrested by the Mexican police.

In court, the prosecution argued that Baines and Jonson were handing over information that would be extremely useful to the Russians. Did this so-called 'useful' information include the decoded messages taken from Baines's own machine, telling the Russians that their very own submarines were undergoing trials in the Arctic Ocean?

Spying, Old and New

A spy can find out information vital to his country's security. In World War II, for example, French Resistance workers were able to discover the location of German rocket sites. Those rocket sites were raining high explosives on the British Isles, and the British government desperately wanted them destroyed. The Royal Air Force had the planes and bombs – the French Resistance knew the locations. The problem was communication. How could the French in enemy territory pass the information on to Britain?

They had radios, but the Germans were constantly searching for their hiding places. If caught, Resistance radio operators would be tortured until they revealed the names of their comrades and the structure of the Resistance network.

Spying in a foreign country was therefore an extremely dangerous business. Spy satellites like Rhyolite represented a great step forward. However, a spy satellite couldn't break into a foreign safe and steal secret papers. Human agents in foreign countries were still essential.

Satellite links between agents and CIA headquarters in the USA had been possible before 1973, but they could only be used at certain times of the day – when the satellite was in range – and could be listened to by the enemy or the agent! The problem was to protect those agents from discovery.

That was what Pyramider was set up to do.

The CIA wrote to the defence company and asked them to come up with a scheme for contacting their spies anywhere in the world.

They asked for a system that would:

1 **protect the agent from being caught by radio tracking devices**

2 **work without the need for land-based radio stations in foreign countries**

3 **allow many different types of messages to be sent at the same time**

4 **enable an agent to communicate at any time without delay and from anywhere in the world**

5 **be secure against enemy powers reading the messages or tracing the sender**

It was an incredible idea. A spy could be in the heart of a foreign country and he (or she) could take out a transmitter disguised as a pocket calculator, a cigarette case or a torch, and talk to his base in the USA. It would truly be like something from a James Bond movie.

A year before Mike Baines arrived at the defence company, a team of 40 engineers succeeded in designing a system that would do all the CIA wanted.

Pyramider would need three satellites, each in orbit 35,000 km above the Earth – one would be over the Indian Ocean, one over the Pacific and one over South-east Asia. Whichever satellite the secret agent contacted, it could pass on his message to the other satellites in a relay that ended in CIA headquarters.

The radio signals would be safe because they would be 'hidden' amongst normal radio station frequencies.

As Mike Baines's defence counsel pointed out at his trial, none of the skills needed to assemble Pyramider was secret. It was simply that no one had ever assembled the right team or been willing to invest millions of dollars to create such a communication network.

The defence company planners calculated that Pyramider would cost between 350 and 450 million dollars. It was this that caused the CIA problems. The CIA did not think the US government would give them the money. The project was 'shelved', and the plans locked away.

What happened next changed the course of Mike Baines's life.

THE COLD WAR

Baines's spying can only be understood in the context of its time, when the West (the USA, Britain and West Germany among others) and the Communist Bloc (Russia, China and East Germany) were striving to outdo each other in the nuclear arms race. His treachery, in other words, took place against the backdrop of the Cold War.

The Cold War was the long period of intense rivalry between Communist and non-Communist nations that lasted from the years after World War II to the fall of the Berlin Wall in 1989. It earned its name from the fact that outright ('hot') hostilities — especially nuclear ones — fortunately never broke out.

The conflict originated with the refusal of Russian leader Josef Stalin to honour the so-called Declaration on United Europe (1945) — a document 'guaranteeing' free elections in the Eastern European countries his forces liberated from Nazi occupation. Instead, Stalin installed puppet governments answerable to him, effectively dividing the continent in two. The British Prime Minister Winston Churchill said famously that "an iron curtain" had descended across Europe.

To hold back Communist expansion, the West resorted to a 'containment' policy, closing borders and lining them with military forces. Nevertheless, tension rose in 1948 with the West's establishment of the German Federal Republic (West Germany) – Russia responded with a blockade of the German city of Berlin. For 11 months the Western powers airlifted food and supplies into West Berlin. The blockade was lifted only after the formation of the Communist-governed German Democratic Republic (East Germany).

In 1949, Russia tested its first nuclear bomb (the West already had a nuclear capability). This increased – if that were possible – the fear and mistrust between the sides. It also coincided with the Communist Revolution in China.

The tension had to break. When it did, it was not as feared in Europe, but across the world in Korea when the Communist-backed North attacked the Western-backed South. Remote as Korea seemed, world nuclear war was only narrowly averted. The conclusion of the conflict saw the Korean Peninsula still divided; however, both the USA and Russia had received a scare, and were now determined to live in what was dubbed 'peaceful co-existence'.

Over the next 40 years, a pattern emerged that was entirely typical of the Cold War: periods of warmer relations between the two blocs, or 'thaws', were followed by those of deep 'freeze'. Tensions between East and West, for example, were heightened by the

Hungarian Uprising (1956), the building of the Berlin Wall (1961), the Cuban Missile Crisis (1962), the Russian Invasion of Czechoslovakia (1968), and American involvement in the Vietnam War (from the early 1960s to 1975). 'Thaws' included treaties banning the testing of nuclear weapons in the atmosphere or outer space; the setting-up of a 'hotline' between the Russian premier and the US President to reduce the chance of accidental nuclear war; increased trade; and arms limitation talks.

Such advances in understanding, minimal though they seemed, were once again frozen with the Russian invasion of Afghanistan in 1979. The difference here was that, while the US could once again increase its spending on arms massively, Russia was bankrupt: it simply could not afford to compete in the arms race. Realizing the hopelessness of the situation, the new Russian premier Mikhail Gorbachev decided to turn his back on the past and allow limited democracy and freedom of expression within his country. At the same time relations with the West were improved, and the reins held on Eastern European countries loosened. Finally in 1988 the Russian army began to withdraw from Afghanistan.

Ironically, it was these first glimmers of liberalism that brought about the collapse of the Communist Bloc. The demolition in 1989 of the Berlin Wall – that symbol of a divided

Europe – was the signal for Eastern European countries to secede entirely from Russian control; in 1991 the former Soviet Union itself broke up into a number of independent, non-Communist states.

These events may have marked the end of the Cold War, and even of the kind of Cold War-style espionage Mike Baines was involved in; but it is unlikely to mean the end of espionage. Secrets might no longer affect the "fate of nations", but there will always be a market for traitors to trade in.

Star Wars

Just three years after Mike Baines escaped from Lompoc, President Reagan announced that the USA would invest in an ambitious satellite defence programme. Satellites would hover in space and watch the skies; if a missile headed towards the USA then the satellite would use a laser cannon to shoot it down. The world was amazed at the announcement of the Strategic Defence Initiative (SDI) and quickly nick-named the project 'Star Wars'.

The concept of Star Wars was far more dramatic than even Pyramider. On March 23, 1983, President Reagan told the world what the US planned to do: he claimed a Star Wars defence of satellite gunships could put an end to all wars – no one would be foolish enough to start a war against America if they were sure to lose.

The President spoke of offering the world a vision of hope and said the SDI holds the promise of changing the course of human history.

President Reagan was praised for revealing America's plans, while Mike Baines was sentenced to 40 years in prison!

THE NUCLEAR SHIELD

President Reagan's Star Wars 'vision of hope' was never built. It was simply too expensive. Pyramider was shelved because it would have cost around half a billion dollars; Star Wars research alone was to cost 30 billion!

Then, at the end of the 1980s, the former Soviet Union broke up into smaller, less threatening states. There no longer seemed to be any reason to spend those hundreds of billions of dollars.

President Bush, who succeeded Reagan, reduced SDI to the curious GPALS (Global Protection Against Limited Strikes). President Clinton then cut the budget back by an enormous 50 per cent.

Nuclear defences were being run down as the danger of nuclear war seemed to recede. However, exactly 13 years after Reagan's Star Wars speech, the idea was revived by the former British Prime Minister, Margaret Thatcher.

She discussed the following points with several world leaders:

1 **The collapse of the Soviet Union made the dangers of nuclear attack *greater* not less. Now several smaller states had missiles.**

2 **The CIA had conducted a survey of**

missiles around the world, using systems like Rhyolite to get their information. They discovered that many small countries had missiles – some not friendly to the USA and Europe.

3   The CIA report claimed, "Of the nations that have acquired weapons of mass destruction, many are led by megalomaniacs and strongmen of proven inhumanity or by weak, unstable governments."

4   The missiles could be armed with chemical warheads (spreading poisoned gas), biological warheads (spreading disease) or nuclear warheads.

5   What was needed was a strong satellite defence system of the kind proposed by Ronald Reagan.

In a curious way, Ronald Reagan was proved right when he said the Star Wars proposal would change the course of human history. The Russians realized they could never match US technology in building a satellite laser system, and that they couldn't afford such a system anyway (Russia was practically bankrupt). Added to a number of other factors including internal unrest, this precipitated the break-up of the former Soviet Union.

The Third Man

Baines and Jonson were not the only traitors in the West selling satellite secrets to the Russians in the 1970s. Across the Atlantic a spy called Geoffrey Arthur Prime, who worked in Britain's GCHQ (Government Communication Headquarters), was busy taking photographs of top secret documents and despatching these to Soviet contacts in East Germany.

Prime was an RAF sergeant who developed Communist sympathies in the mid-1960s. He learned Russian and in 1968, while on leave in Berlin, contacted the Russian authorities. Back in Britain he applied successfully for a job in GCHQ's language service.

Prime's Russian paymasters took his position seriously enough to give him extensive training in the arts of espionage. They provided him with specially treated carbon paper which, when written on, produced invisible writing on the paper beneath. They instructed him in the techniques of miniature photography, giving him a tiny Minox-B camera to produce 'microdots' (photographic negatives the size of a full-stop). They even issued him with a false-bottomed leather briefcase! His Russian code name was to be Rowlands.

Prime took his instructions from the KGB

by tuning in to East German radio and noting down long rows of code numbers read out at specified times of the day. From 1969 to 1975 he photographed such things as GCHQ's internal telephone directory, transcripts of telephone calls, high-frequency and microwave voice communications, and lists of key words and code names.

In 1976, at the same time as Baines and Jonson were selling satellite secrets to the Russians in Mexico, documents relating to Rhyolite passed through GCHQ. Prime realized the importance of these and immediately sent off a message to his controllers in East Germany. A meeting was quickly arranged in Vienna, Austria, and Prime was able to take with him highly sensitive photos of the new material, and even a number of pages of the top secret documents concerned.

When Baines and Jonson were caught in 1977, Prime followed their trials closely. He feared he might meet a similar fate, though his controllers assured him that, should he ever decide to defect to Russia, he would be given the rank of colonel in the KGB and a lifelong pension.

Prime, however, resolved to take matters into his own hands. Pleading pressure of work, in September 1977 he resigned from GCHQ. Instead of defecting, however, he took a job as a taxi driver. At last he thought himself free of his dangerous double life. Ironically, it was his arrest in 1982 for an entirely unrelated offence that exposed his spying career.

Searching Prime's rooms for evidence of that offence, police stumbled by chance on his spy kit and code book. After an initial refusal to co-operate, the spy confessed. In the course of a short trial the court heard the whole saga of his 10 years as a 'mole' (a traitor working from within a government organization). Following the inevitable guilty verdict, the judge told Prime: "You made the choice, and you must suffer". With that, he sentenced him to 38 years in prison.

On the Run

Within a month of Mike Baines's escape from Lompoc in early 1980, doubts were expressed about the *Escape from Alcatraz* story (one source even described it as 'hogwash'). Prisoners said the dummy head ruse would never work: guards had to check the cells thoroughly and touch a prisoner's skin or see a moving body. Mike Baines, the prisoners claimed, must have had keys and outside help.

Whatever the case, in June 1980, FBI investigators followed up rumours that he was in Mexico. However, the trail soon went cold. In October 1980, an ex-convict called Douglas Wargo told the *New York Times* that he had met Mike Baines several times since his escape nine months before. Police raided Wargo's house but found nothing – they'd missed Baines by some nine hours.

Wargo then confessed he'd taken a package of documents from Baines in Lima, Peru. He'd delivered them to a man with a 'Russian-sounding voice'. It seemed Baines had managed to hide Dungeon documents in the Arizona desert before his arrest. He'd unearthed them after his escape – and sold yet another secret to the Russians.

The CIA and FBI hunt for Baines became ever more intense. The Wargo package had apparently contained sensitive 'KH-11' documents, which suggests they were genuine: the CIA admitted KH stood for Keyhole – a spy camera device.

Some 1981 newspaper reports show that Baines was as skilled at disinformation as the CIA. There were tales of him appearing all over the American continent. In February he was said to be smuggling arms to Nicaragua and El Salvador from Cuba; he was also 'seen' in Mexico and Costa Rica, where he was reported to be selling ancient historical items! The FBI didn't swallow these stories. However, there was another tale they were only too happy to believe.

A year after Baines's escape, it was reported that a man from New Jersey had helped him to flee to Southern Africa. Frank Abbott Sweeney, a fraudster and bank robber who had served time with Baines in Stone Island, was followed for months by police in the hope he might lead them to the fugitive. In May 1981 they intercepted letters Sweeney had written to another inmate in Lompoc prison. One of the letters said: "Two marshals interviewed me yesterday about our escaped friend. Somehow they have discovered that I helped him into South Africa. In fact they have managed to pinpoint the exact area. I suspect an informer has been at work. If the FBI contact you, say nothing."

This letter at first seemed a credible pointer to Baines's whereabouts. Sweeney had many contacts in Africa, and had even served as a mercenary in the Rhodesian army.

In fact, as the FBI soon discovered, the letter was written by Sweeney to throw them off his friend's trail. For Baines, Sweeney eventually revealed, was still running free somewhere in the USA.

Embarrassed and disappointed though they were, federal agents did not have to wait long before recapturing the Russian spy. On August 21 of that year, acting on a tip-off from an anonymous source, Baines was arrested in a hamburger bar at Port Angeles, a coastal fishing village 80 kilometres north of Seattle, Washington State. He had been on the run for one and a half years; how had he managed to survive? The story that emerged proved every bit as sensational as that of his spying activities.

Baines had spent the past year robbing banks!

It appeared that, after breaking out from Lompoc, Baines spent a few weeks hiding in the desert area nearby, sleeping in the open and eating insects and wild berries. He then made his way north to Washington State where, under the alias Jim Namchek, he camped out near the town of Bonner's Ferry. According to residents, he lived alone for a time in a tent in the mountains, using a mule to transport supplies to his camp site.

Soon, however, he made contact with a Mrs Gloria White, who operated a hideout for outlaws. Criminals left her home periodically to rob banks, returning to share out their loot. At Mrs White's 'safe house' Baines formed a partnership with Calvin Robinson (also a former inmate of Lompoc), who instructed him in the techniques of armed robbery. Together they went on a robbing spree across Idaho, Montana and Washington, stealing more than $27,000. Mrs White aided and abetted the pair, helping to prepare disguises such as false beards and sharing in the proceeds of the bank jobs.

After a time, however, fearing their activities were drawing too much police attention, Baines decided to move to Washington State's remote Olympic Peninsula. Here, living under the aliases Tony Lester and Sean Hennessey, he bought a boat and attempted to start a fishing business.

He might have stayed free, too, but for his betrayal by the unnamed source from Bonner's Ferry.

On January 13, 1982, after being held for some months in a high security police cell, Baines pleaded guilty to charges of armed robbery. He went into court facing a possible sentence of up to 90 years in prison and a $60,000 fine.

During the course of the trial, government agents argued that some of the money from the hold-ups was going to help Baines defect to Russia. However, little evidence was produced to confirm this.

On May 1, 1982, Baines was sentenced to 25 years in prison. Judge Hal Ryan ordered him to begin serving this sentence when he had completed the 40 years he received in 1977 for selling US secrets to the Russians.

Before he was led away, a stunned Baines said to reporters, "I never meant to harm anyone, and I never did."

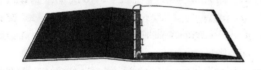

Epilogue

If Mike Baines *was* working for the CIA or
the KGB, then it would seem neither helped
him after his escape from Lompoc. He was
forced into bank robbery – not a very
appropriate activity, you might think, for a spy.

While on the run, Baines was said to have
phoned a newspaper reporter from an
airport. He wouldn't say where he was calling
from or where he was headed but, questioned
about his escape from a high security prison,
he insisted the *Escape from Alcatraz* story
was true. He described crawling through the
fences at Lompoc and said, "My knees were
shaking. I thought I was going to get a bullet
in the head."

The reporter then asked, "There's a lot of
talk that your escape was organized by the
KGB or the CIA. Can you tell me which it
was?"

Baines laughed and said, "I did it by myself."

Despite this, some people continue to
believe Baines's escape was part of an
elaborate conspiracy.

At the end of the seven minute phone
conversation, Baines asked the reporter to
pass on his love to his mother and father. "I
never felt better. I love to be free," he added.

He may never be able to say that again –
or will he?

CLASSIFIED

YOU CAN'T HIDE THE TRUTH FOREVER

Reader, your brief is to be alert for the following spine-tingling books.

Break Out!	Terry Deary	978 0 7534 1535 1	£4.9
Discovery at Roswell	Terry Deary	978 0 7534 1533 7	£4.9
The Nuclear Winter Man	Terry Deary	978 0 7534 1534 4	£4.9
Vanished!	Terry Deary	978 0 7534 1532 0	£4.9